Alfred John Church

The Legend of Saint Vitalis

And other poems

Alfred John Church

The Legend of Saint Vitalis
And other poems

ISBN/EAN: 9783337152727

Printed in Europe, USA, Canada, Australia, Japan

Cover: Foto ©Andreas Hilbeck / pixelio.de

More available books at **www.hansebooks.com**

THE

LEGEND OF SAINT VITALIS

AND OTHER POEMS

BY

ALFRED J. CHURCH, M.A.

AUTHOR OF 'STORIES FROM HOMER,' ETC.

Oxford

B. H. BLACKWELL, BROAD STREET

—◆—

LONDON: SEELEY & CO., ESSEX STREET, STRAND

MDCCLXXXVII

PREFACE.

THESE few verses are all that I have been able to do towards realizing one of the dreams of my life, the winning a place, though it were but the 'lowest room,' among English poets. They have been written at rare intervals during a period of nearly forty years; and I cannot now expect the health, the spirits, or the leisure by which I might accomplish more. My excuse for collecting them is the hope that among them may possibly be found one or two worthy to live.

Most of the pieces have been published in the *Spectator*, and I thank my kind friends, the proprietors of that journal, for the permission to

reprint them. "The Sea of Galilee" obtained
the "Prize for a Poem on a Sacred Subject" at
Oxford in 1883. The last two stanzas have been
repeated and expanded in "A Christmas Hope."
I should have omitted them but that it seemed
right to print a prize poem substantially as it
stood when it was submitted to the judges. The
translation of "Could we forget the widowed
hour" from *In Memoriam* appeared in a volume
entitled *Horae Tennysonianae* which I had the
honour of editing. It is now out of print, thanks,
not to any urgent demand from the public, but to
a fire which consumed the edition. The translation was praised by Charles Stuart Calverley, and
this is my reason for reprinting it.

A. C.

Hadley, *Dec.* 27, 1886.

CONTENTS.

	PAGE
The Legend of S. Vitalis	1
The Sea of Galilee	6
Elijah	14
A Hope	18
All Saints Day	22
All Saints and All Souls	23
Unseen	26
Accident	28
The Bracelet	30
A Regret	32
The Ebb of Love	34
England and Sebastopol	36
Nepenthe	37
Charles Gordon	39
In Memoriam Puellulæ Dulcissimæ	41
In Memoriam William Brownrigg Smith	44
On the Death of a Dog	46
The Tapestry of Proserpine	50
The Dream-Lovers	53
Hecuba and Agamemnon	56
'Could we forget the widowed hour'	60

THE LEGEND OF S. VITALIS.

VITALIS stood before his cell and mused;
    ' "Of women cometh wickedness," so spake
Jesus the son of Sirach, speaking truth.
I thank Thee, Lord, that Thou hast led my feet
Far from the perilous ways wherein they stand
Watching for souls of men, for, since I closed
My mother's eyes in death, I have not looked
On face of woman, and my heart is fixed
Not to regard it till the day I die.'
And peace was in his soul; but ere he slept
He read the Gospel,—how the woman stood
Behind the Christ, and washed His feet with tears,
And wiped them with her hair; and all the night
Christ seemed to walk beside him in his dreams
Through the great sinful city: foul of tongue,

Bare-bosomed, evil-eyed, the women thronged;
But He, with boundless yearning in His eyes,
Pointed, and said, 'My sisters,—shall they die?'
And the monk woke, and thought, 'It is a snare';
But night by night he found the dream return,
And ever saw within the yearning eyes
A mightier love, and heard the pleading voice
Broken with tears; so, after counsel sought
Of him who ruled the house, Vitalis went.

Much mused he going how the work might speed,
And doubted much, and, when he reached the town,
Stood in the turmoil as a man amazed.
Then wandering, as it seemed, with aimless foot,
Came to a quay from which they loaded wheat
On corn-ships bound for Rome. A sailor cried,
Mocking his garb, 'Ho? sluggard, wilt thou work?'
And the rough voice was as the voice of God,
Scattering his doubt, for all the day he worked
Hard, as for life, then going, wage in hand,
Found one who issued to her evil trade,

And gave, and whispered, 'From thy brother Christ ;
Sin not to-night'; then followed to her house,
Heedless what men might say, and, while she slept,
Wrestled with prayer and weeping for her soul.

So did he many days, but some, who saw
The man go to and fro in evil haunts,
Thought shame, and spake him roughly, ' Break thy vows,
False monk, in honest wedlock, if thou must,
Nor drag the robe of Christ in filthy ways.'
But he was silent, or with brief reply,
' To my own Lord I answer,' went his way ;
For much he feared lest they, the thrice accursed,
Who live by others' sin, should mar the work.
But not the less—for never yet was maid
That shrank from ill with keener pang of shame—
The iron pierced his soul, and all his cry,
Save but for those the lost ones whom he sought,
Was ever this,—'Lord, let my cause be known ;
Let Thy word try me, living, Lord, or dead,—
All as Thou wilt, so only all be known.'

And oft at noon-day, in the pause of toil,
His thoughts unbidden travelled to the home
Of the old peaceful days, the rock-built cell,
The garden in the ledges of the cliff,
With melon gay and pulse and climbing gourd;
And the great desert sleeping in the sun,
Changelessly calm; and 'neath the furthest sky,
The green Nile-watered fields and shining stream.

But at the last it chanced, that, coming forth
From some ill-famed abode, a passer-by
Espied and smote him, harder than he wot;
And he, as knowing that the end was come,
Cried, 'Man, thou smitest sore, but all the town
Shall hear the blow which I will smite thee back.'
Then staggered, bleeding, wounded to the death,
To such mean chamber as he called his own.
But one poor wanderer, whom his love had brought
To life from paths of death, had marked the deed;
And her nor oath of silence, nor the thought
How all her shameful past must spring to light,

Kept, but she told her tale; and every word,
Heard through the stormy passion of her sobs,
Pierced as a dagger to the striker's heart,
Till grovelling on the ground, 'O Lord!' he cried.
' Forgive me, I have slain thy sweetest saint.'
Then rose and hasted, seeking for the monk,—
And the crowd grew behind him as he ran.
Dead on his knees they found him, with a scroll
Whereon was writ, with hand that failed in death,
Judge nought before the time, till Christ shall come,
Bringing to day the hidden things of night,
And making plain the counsels of the heart.

And when they buried him, behind the bier
Walked Patriarch, priests, and nobles, as was meet ;
And a great throng of women, happy wives,
And mothers blest in wedlock-bands, and some,
Vowed servants of the Church, for Christ had won
His sisters, and the monk had worked his work.

(The story may be found in Mr. Baring-Gould's *Lives of the Saints,*
January.)

THE SEA OF GALILEE.

Galilace, vicisti.

AMONG the many-tinted hills it lies,
   'Deep Galilee,' like a sapphire which a queen
Wears on her breast, amid the gorgeous dyes,
   Glory of Eastern looms, and lustrous sheen
Of woven gold ; while deep with kindred hue
Arches above the cloudless Syrian blue.

Fair as of old it lies, but sad, and lone,
   And lifeless,—only wheeling from the cliff
The cormorant cries, and on some wave-washed stone
   The crane stands watching, or some fisher's skiff
Spreads on the vacant waters to the gale
The solitary whiteness of a sail.

Or, haply, journeyed from some Western land,
  At the wave's edge a stranger reins his steed ;
Among his desert riders see him stand,
  Gazing with eyes far rapt, that seem to heed
Nought but the Presence which divinely fills
Green earth, and shimmering lake, and purple hills.

Earth has no holier spot,—not where the Maid
  Bowed her meek head to hear from Gabriel's lips
Her high espousals, nor where He was laid
  Whose uncreated glory bare eclipse
In the frail childhood of a man, nor where
He drained with mighty agonies of prayer

The cup of His great passion, nor the Hill,
  Surnamed of death, on whose dark brow He gave
His life to the destroyers, to fulfil
  The world's great ransom, nor that empty grave
From which streams forth for ever on the night
Of worlds unseen Hope's unextinguished light.

Earth's holiest spot,—yet not for marvels wrought,
  Though on these shores, where proud Capernaum's
    head
Lies low in dust, to paths of life He brought
  The unreturning footsteps of the dead;
Though here still roll the self-same waves that grew
Calm at His footsteps; though the winds that knew,

Hushed to swift peace, the bidding of their Lord;
  Rush fierce as ever from the circling hills;
And, where the gently sloping heights afford
  A larger space, the watchful love that fills
All things that live immediate bade appear
For instant need the bounties of the year.

Here dwell the memories of His earthly days,
  Of that fair Presence, full of truth and grace,
In which, attempered to our mortal gaze,
  The Eternal Glory shone, while, face to face,
Man talked with God, in grasp of human hands
Feeling the Love by which Creation stands;

Here to the littleness, not all unsweet,
  Of daily needs He stooped; here shared the talk
That ripples kindly on where comrades meet
  For meal, or noonday rest, or evening walk;
Here deigned to feel, while all things owned Him Lord,
Heart drawn to heart in friendship's sweet accord.

O mightiest friendship since the world began!
  Mark by yon shore, of lowly garb and mien,
Slow pacing, rapt in thought, that lonely man,
  A son of toil, a nameless Nazarene;
This hour His mission calls Him, He shall take
Publican, peasant, fisher of the lake,—

Weak natures, apt to fear, and narrow souled,—
  And He shall teach them greatness; they shall grow
His presence shaping, to heroic mould;
  Shall wield the mystic arms that overthrow
The strongholds built of evil, and shall find
The secret of the keys that loose and bind.

Such were the partner brothers; all the night
  Still saw the favourable moonlight gleam
On empty nets, till rolling thick and white
  The mists of morning gathered, and the beam
Of earliest sunrise showed its rosy light
O'er Gilead's hill and Bashan's oak-clad height.

Then, as they turned them shoreward, One, who cried
  With voice of strange, sweet, mastering command,
Bade cast again upon the nearer side;
  Now such the shoal, they scarce can win the land.
Then, while they count and wonder, 'Ye shall be
Fishers of men,' He said, ' but follow Me.'

Fishers of men! who would not rather stay
  Content to win the waters' glittering spoil,
Careless to ply the labours of the day,
  Careless to sleep the dreamless sleep of toil,
Till, toil and slumber ended, by his grave
Shall plash unheard the long familiar wave?

Fishers of men! what perilous seas ye dare!
  What hidden treachery of shoal and rock!
What toil of adverse winds! what dull despair
  Of stagnant calm! what dread of tempest shock!
What pain of wasted night and fruitless day!
How wild the waters, and how fierce the prey!

Yet go! ye bear your Master o'er the deep.
  Shall they who carry such a Cæsar fear?
Go, for He watches, though He seem to sleep,
  And when ye think Him distant, He is near.
Ready, through blackest night and loudest storm,
To show the radiant Presence of His form.

Lo! ye shall leave Him, ye shall watch Him die,
  As dies some felon slave; but death shall seal
The unfinished pact of life, and bind the tie
  It seems to loose for ever; ye shall feel
A mightier Presence, and shall nearer draw
To Him ye see not, than to Him ye saw.

So shall ye conquer till the Jew disclaim
  His haughty saintship, till the Greek shall own
His long-sought wisdom found; the Name ye name
  Shall quell the ravening eagles that have flown
From Roman hills o'er either world, and draw
Barbarian chaos to the sway of law.

Not this your triumph, that the future brings
  Days when the Pontiff Fisherman shall shine
In Cæsar's purple, and on necks of kings
  Shall plant the foot of lordship; more divine
The kingdom that ye fight for, it shall win
Spirits and souls of men, and rule within.

This is thy lesson, Lake of Galilee!
  Not from the seats of Empire,—lordly Nile,
Tiber, or proud Euphrates,—but from thee,
  Fair lake, that knowest but to frown or smile
As skies are calm or angry, springs the power
That rules the world till Time's supremest hour.

The towers of stone shall crumble, and the wall
  Lie level as the plain; thy sea and sky
Change not, O Lake! while Empires rise and fall,
  Types of the changeless faith that shall not die,
Though all things human fail it, till the Son
See in a world restored the Eternal Purpose won.

And when the great time-cycles bring to nought
  The births of Time, by instant change or slow,—
Whether it fall that what the years have wrought
  The years undo, or instant-kindled glow
Of solar fires dissolve this solid frame,
Sudden as raindrop in a furnace-flame,

Thy glory still endures, for He that trod
  Thy shores of old hath set, beyond the range
Of mortal ebb and flow, secure in God
  The manhood that He bare, and over Change,
Mighty world-conqueror, and destroying Time,
A Galilean victor, sits sublime.

ELIJAH.

Fragments of an uncompleted poem.

*   *   *   *   *   *   *   *

The children's wail, the strong man's dumb despair
Smote on his soul. All daily sights and sounds,
Distressful lowings of the herds that lay
Spent by the dusty pools, the blighted fields,
And Gilead's royal forests all discrowned,
Reproached him. Wherefore far from haunts of men,
Where Cherith flows by Ammon's furthest bound,
He dwelt remote, and waited. Not alone
He dwelt, whose solitude was populous
With signs of God, and table daily spread
By Him who makes the wilderness abound
With plenty of the mart, and lays command
On all things, stormy wind and flaming fire,
And beast and feathered fowl, to serve His will.

*   *   *   *   *   *   *   *

'Let him that troubleth Israel stand accursed!'
Aye—but who is he? Not the man who wakes
A nation brain-benumbed with opiate draughts
Of pleasure, pointing to the lurid clouds
Where fires of vengeance gather, not the voice
That shakes the tyrannies of wrong, or bares
Veiled oracles of falsehood to the day;
Not these, but rather he who whispers 'Peace'
Where peace is not, who prophesies deceits,
Who feeds with lies high-swollen lusts of power,
Or smooths the path of folly till it end
Abrupt in some sheer precipice of doom.

*   *   *   *   *   *   *   *

Elijah went up by a whirlwind into Heaven.—2 Kings ii. 11.

So passed the prophet, rapt from mortal eyes,
And saw not death: to what serener air,
What nobler work translated, passes all
God grants of knowledge,—only this we know:
Who stands while God prepares his judgment-day,

And in the dawn that seems to other eyes
Mere darkness bears his witness to the light,
Stands in his spirit and power; who cries, ' Prepare,
Make straight the crooked ways of wrong, and raise
Mean things to greatness, and abase the proud,'
His voice is as Elijah's. Such was he,
Greatest of woman-born, the Baptist named,
Whom that stern mother, Solitude, had wrought
To such a steadfast strength, that not the curse
Of priests, or frowning kings, or deadlier rage
Of woman shamed in lust, could stir his soul.
Such he, the Florentine, whose thunders shook
The Mediceän halls, and thrilled the soul
Of slumbering Italy from Alp to sea;
And such the Teuton Great-heart, undismayed,
Whom not the angry Kaiser, where he sat
With prince and prelate, nor the mystic power
Of Peter's triple crown, one hair's-breadth stirred
From that high vantage whence he moved the world.

O England! O my country! if there come
Such voice to thee, in these dark, latter days;
If some stern prophet—and Elijah's God
Has yet His prophets—bid thee cleanse thy house
From foulness that thou knowest, myriad sins
That ease has bred, and faithless pride, and scorn
Of kindred blood, and hatred, child of wrong,
Heed, lest the curse should fall, and topple down
Thy greatness in the dust, for all thy bounds
Stretch from the rising to the setting Sun,
And touch at either Pole the eternal frost.

A HOPE.

I.

SLOWLY we gather and with pain
From many toils a scanty gain
We strive to know, but scant our powers.
And short the time, and strait the bounds,
And ever-unsurmounted towers
The mortal barrier that surrounds
Our being; and the body still,
Imperious slave, betrays the will.
Slowly we gather and with pain,—
But quick the scattering again
Whether it chance the failing brain
Lets slip the treasure it hath won
Through weary days; or sudden blow
Lays the unshattered fabric low,
And all our doing is undone.

II.

Slowly a nation builds its life
From barbarous chaos into law,
And kindly social ties, and awe
Of powers divine. For civil strife
Still opens wide within the walls
The yawning gulf that will not close
Until the noblest victim falls;
Or, fierce without, the shock of foes
In one wild hour of blood o'erthrows
The labour of the patient years;
And if at last the work appears
Complete in stately strength to stand,
Riot with parricidal blow,
Or mad ambition's traitor hand,
Fierce clutching at the tyrant's crown,
In headlong ruin lays it low,
Or brute battalions tread it down,
Or ease and luxury and sin,
Fell cankers sown of peace, devour,

Till trappings of imperial power
But hide the living death within.

III.

But doubtless growth repairs decay,
And still the great world grows to more,
Though men and nations pass away.
But what if at the source of day
Some cosmic change exhaust the store
Which feeds the myriad forms of life?
What if some unimagined strife
Should raise so high the solar fire,
That all this solid earthly frame
Should in as brief a space expire
As rain-drops in a furnace-flame?

IV.

Yet, if our faith is not the scheme
Of priestly cunning, nor a dream
Which with some fair illusion caught
Our ungrown Manhood's childish thought;

If Christmas tells us true, 'To-day
The Child Divine in Bethlehem lay';
If He is Man who, past the ken
Of Science in her widest range,
Orders the law of ceaseless change,
Content we know that lives of men
Pass as the leaves of spring away,—
That time will bring its final day
To the great world itself, secure
The Eternal Manhood shall endure.

ALL SAINTS DAY.

THEY passed before; they trod the way we tread,
   A way of weary travel, but their eyes
Still strained to see through depth of gloomy skies
The flashing gates of pearl. All tears they shed
   Are changed to deathless blossoms on our way,
All precious drops their wounded feet have bled
Light like fair lamps the lonely path we tread ;
   And still. but most upon this holy day,
They hover near, and swell our faltering song,
   And waft our humble litanies on high,
And bring us near to God. Faint heart, be strong,
   Nor shun the lightened toil. Behold, the sky
Throws wide its portals, and the white-robed throng
Reach forth their hands, and cry, ‘Why tarry ye so long?’

ALL SAINTS AND ALL SOULS.

Many are called, but few are chosen.

THERE are who find their life's delight,
    O Lord! in Thee, on whom Thy grace
Sets from the womb the halo-light
    They wear that see Thy nearer face.

And some, with sudden, strong surprise,
    That masters sin and hate and pride,
Thou takest, as through parted skies
    When Saul beheld the Crucified.

Thou choosest, and they hear Thee call,
    For still Thou wilt not dwell alone;
These are Thy saints, O Lord! but all
    The souls Thou makest are Thine own.

Too well we know they pass Thee by,
  Nor hear Thy voice, so fierce the din
The world without them makes, the cry
  Of passion calls so loud within.

But must they walk the downward way
  To those dark gates, whereon despair
Is writ, nor see again the day?
  Will no wild agonies of prayer

Reach to the seats of peace, and break
  The calm of heaven's harmonious days?
No far-off sound of wailing make
  A discord in the eternal praise?

Oh! yet we trust Thy love, and Him,
  The blessed Christ, who works Thy will,
Who once through trackless regions dim
  Of Hades passed, and rules them still,

Nor rests, nor weary grows, nor faints,
  Till all His royal work be done,—
Till added to Thy first-fruit saints
  The harvest of Thy souls be won.

UNSEEN.

AT the spring of an arch, in the great north tower,
  High up on the wall, is an angel's head,
With, carven beneath it, a lily flower,
  And delicate wings at the side outspread.

They say that the sculptor wrought from the face,
  From the shrouded face of his promised bride,
And, when he had added the last sad grace
  To the features, he dropped his chisel and died.

And the worshippers throng to the shrine below,
  And the sight-seers come with their curious eyes;
But deep in the shadow, where none may know
  Its beauty, the gem of his carving lies.

Yet at early morn on a midsummer day,
  When the sun is far to the north, for the space
Of a few short minutes, there falls a ray,
  Through an amber pane, on the angel's face.

It was wrought for the eye of God, and it seems
  That He blesses the work of the dead man's hand
With a gleam of the golden light that streams
  On the lost that are found in the deathless land.

ACCIDENT.

WHAT strange, unreasoned impulse takes
    By devious ways our aimless feet,
  The unimagined doom to meet?
For still the fatal thunder breaks

From skies that promise peace. We go,
  Scarce e'en on trivial errand bent,
  And heed not, and the stroke is sent
That lays life's pleasant fabric low,—

Long days of dear domestic peace,
  Love into closer union grown,
  The newer knowledge made our own,
And ever, as the years increase,

Some clearer height of wisdom won,
  And schemes of joyous travel planned
  To holy place or classic land,
Or marvel of the midnight sun, —

All things that counterchange our days
  With varied light of toil and ease, —
  Laborious joys, and cares that please,
Constraint of duty, sweets of praise ;

One step, and over love and light,
  Things hoped and things achieved, the all
  We are and were to be, will fall
The mornless, unremembering night.

THE BRACELET.

CLEAR were the heavens when I kissed
   The bracelet on her taper wrist,
Five jacinths and an amethyst.

And, as we lingered, in the height
Through purple depths of summer night
Shone twinkling points of starry light;

And all things round were hushed and still,
But through the hazel-copse a rill
Still murmured, and one passionate thrill

Of song from some late nightingale
With music mixed of love and wail
Flooded the hollows of the dale.

O sunrise dim with mist and cloud!
O head in speechless sorrow bowed!
O golden hair in leaden shroud!

The bird has sought a warmer sky;
The copse is felled; the rill is dry;
I sit alone; but, till I die,

There still will gleam through tearful mist
A bracelet on a taper wrist,
Five jacinths and an amethyst.

A REGRET.

I BLAME not that your courage failed,
    That prudence over love prevailed;
It seemed that we must walk together
Rough ways through wild and stormy weather,
And you must have smooth paths to tread,
And skies all cloudless overhead.

Wise was your choice the world will say,
That sees you fresh and fair to-day
As in the spring-time of your years,
Those hazel eyes undimmed with tears,
That forehead all unlined with care,
Nor streaked with gray that chestnut hair.

Yet if you could have dared to lay
Unfaltering hands in mine, and say,
' I trust you still, nor count the cost!'
Something, I doubt not, you had lost,
Yet found, when all was told, remain
To you and me some larger gain.

Not loveless nor unsweet my days ;
I toil, nor miss some meed of praise ;
Had you been with me they had known
The grace they lack, and thou hadst grown,
O weak but pure and tender heart!
To something nobler than thou art.

THE EBB OF LOVE.

A LOVE that wanes is as an ebbing tide,
Which slowly, inch by inch, and scarce perceived,
With many a wave that makes brave show to rise,
Fails from the shore. No sudden treason turns
The long-accustomed loyalty to hate,
But years bring weariness for sweet content,
And fondness, daily sustenance of love,
Which use should make a tribute easier paid,
First grudged, and then withholden, starves the heart;
And though compassion, or remorseful thoughts
Of happy days departed, bring again
The ancient tenderness in seeming flood,
Not less it ebbs and ebbs till all is bare.

O happy shore, the flowing tide shall brim
Thy empty pools, and spread dull tangled weeds
In streamers many-coloured as the lights
Which flash in northern heavens, and revive
The fainting blossoms of the rocks ; but thou,
O heart, whence love hath ebbed, art ever bare!

ENGLAND AND SEBASTOPOL, 1854.

THE moon is full; her radiance sleeps
    On field and wood, a silver light:
In hope and fear a maiden keeps
    Her vigil through the silent night.

In thought she sees the splendour fall
    Far, far away on friend and foe,
On sleeping camp and leaguered wall,
    And watchfires burning dim and low,

Where 'neath an Eastern sky he wakes,
    Or, sleeping till he hear the stir
Of moving hosts as morning breaks,
    He starts to arms from dreams of her.

NEPENTHE.

THE north wind follows free and fills
  Our rounding sail, and overhead
Deepens the rainless blue, and red
The sunset burns on quarried hills;

And peace is over all, as deep
  As where, amid the secular gloom
  Of some far-reaching, rock-built tomb,
The nameless generations sleep,

While, undecayed as on the day
  That saw them first, the Kings of old,
  In sculptured calm serene, behold
The slow millenniums pass away.

Still, far behind us, as we cleave
  Smooth-flowing Nile, the din of life
  And passionate voices of the strife
Are hushed to silence, and we leave

The cares that haunt us, dark regret
  For wasted years, and wild unrest,
  Yearning for praise or pleasure, blest
With life's last blessing,—to forget.

For still in Egypt's kindly air,
  Strong antidote of mortal woes,
  The painless herb, Nepenthe, grows,
Which she whom fair-haired Leda bare

Mixed in the wine, and stilled their pain
  Who wept in Spartan halls for sire
  Or brother, wrapped in funeral fire,
Or wandering o'er the boundless main.

CHARLES GORDON.

January 26, 1885.

We trusted it had been he who should have redeemed Israel.

GREAT soul, that scorned ignoble ease,
    Still lit with faith's undying flame,
Great leader, ever prompt to seize
    War's swift occasions as they came!

We hoped thou could'st not fail to save;
    We hoped,—but under alien skies,
Far off, within thy nameless grave,
    Buried the hope of nations lies.

Is this the end? Forbid the thought!
    The servant follows still the Lord,
For each hath death the victory wrought,
    With Him the cross, with thee the sword.

The Saviour dies, betrayed, alone,
  His Israel unredeemed, but still
Grows to a mightier world-wide throne
  The felon cross on Calvary's hill.

Nor thou, great soul, wast spent in vain,
  Though noblest of our later days.
While from the tropic Nile-washed plain
  The echo of thy deathless praise

Shall bring across each petty strife,
  Each base desire, and meaner aim,
The vision of a holier life,
  A loftier purpose, purer fame.

IN MEMORIAM PUELLULÆ DULCISSIMÆ.

D. P. W.

AH! what is left for love to prize?
   A little dress or trinket-toy
Which once could make the innocent eyes
   Brighten with glimpses of the joy
The woman feels in being fair—
   A chair left sadly in its place—
A little tress of chestnut hair—
   A little likeness of her face,
Ah! vacant of the living light
   Which magic sunbeam never gave—
And, on our city's northern height,
   Across a thousand streets—a grave.

No more, no more. O fruitless pain
  Of birth and nurture, wasted years
Of care, and watches watched in vain!
  O idle hopes! O idle fears!

'Tis well to tell us she is blest,
  That never sin or grief shall break
The quiet of her perfect rest.
  O God, but is it well to make
These desolate homes, that round Thy throne
  Haply may stand in denser throng
The children-angels? Must the tone
  Of these pure voices swell the song
That hymns Thee Lord of all, and leave
  These dreadful gaps of silence here?

O Lord, forgive us if we grieve
  Too wildly, if the starting tear
Confuse our vision; make us see
  What steadfast, changeless purpose runs

Through all Thy ways, to bring to Thee,
Or soon or late, Thy wandering sons.
Content if slow they come, for sake
Of those they love, and loath to part
From what Thou givest, Thou dost take
The treasure lest Thou lose the heart.

IN MEMORIAM

WILLIAM BROWNRIGG SMITH.

MARTYRS there are, whose high renown
　　Fills heaven and earth alike, who rise
　On fiery chariot to the skies;
There are who win the martyr's crown

While leading dull, mechanic days,
　　Who, walking in the common round
　　Of meanest duties, still have found
Occasions of divinest praise.

Such was our friend; the many knew
　　His presence, with its genial grace,
　　The low, sweet voice, the kindly face,
They knew him loyal, tender, true.

They knew not all. Erect and calm
    He bore a burden that had bent
    A meaner spirit, still content
To run the race nor ask the palm.

God gave him much, but much denied.
    He had the scholar's deepest lore,
    Nor spurned at fame, yet never wore
The bays that grace a scholar's pride.

God gave him love; with ceaseless care
    One flickering flame of life to tend,
    To watch, to pray, and, when the end
Was come for her, his rest was near.

Rest, dear one, where thine all is known:
    We wander on with weary feet
    Through darkened ways, until we meet,
If meet we may, before the throne.

ON THE DEATH OF A DOG.

LADY, I hold the poet's task
    No wasted pains, though some may say.
'What right has meaner loss to ask
    Our human grief, when every day

That dawns in Eastern skies must make
    On loving lips the passionate kiss
Grow cold for ever, and shall break
    A thousand nearer ties than this?'

Ah! well; but who is wise to know
    How man, the lordly head and crown,
Is finely linked with things below;
    Through what gradations passing down

The common nerve of kindred runs ?
  And if we mourn for something lost,
Whene'er it chance that treacherous suns
  Have leagued with April's lingering frost

To slay the tender blooms of spring,
  Who then shall deem the gift a wrong
To nobler sorrows if we bring
  For such a grave a wreath of song ?

Not only now for something bright,
  A pleasant presence past away,
Not only for the vanished light
  Of hazel eyes you mourn to-day;

Not only that the glancing feet
  Are still in death, that never more
The happy-ringing voice may greet
  Familiar steps upon the floor ;

For something more than common dust
  Was that which clung so close to man,
The heart that still was wise to trust,
  And strong to love; whose pulses ran

An honest current, to the beat
  Of one affection ever true—
Bring, happy springtime, for the sweet
  The sweetest flowers that ever grew;

And thou, lie kindly light on her,
  O gentle earth, whose delicate tread
Thy frailest flower would scarcely stir,
  And softly lap the graceful head.

Can this be all? or shall we deem
  That in the thought of equal skies
Of which some simple soul may dream
  More than an idle fancy lies?

Ah! who shall answer? for we grow
  Confused with darkness, and the veil
Is over all things; this we know,
  · That love is love, and shall not fail.

THE TAPESTRY OF PROSERPINE.

CLAUDIAN, *The Rape of Proserpine*, i. 246-65.

THE elemental order there she drew
    And Jove's high dwellings ; there you saw
The needle tell how ancient Chaos grew
    To harmony and law;

How Nature set in order due and rank
    Her atoms, raised the light on high,
And to the middle place the weightier sank ;
    There lustrous shone the sky,

The heavens were quick with flame, the ocean rolled,
    The great world hung in mid suspense.
Each was of diverse hue ; she worked in gold
    The starry fires intense,

Bade ocean flow in purple, and the shore
    With gems upraised. Divinely wrought,
The threads embossed to swelling billows bore
    Strange likeness; you had thought

They dashed the sea-weed on the rocks, or crept
    Hoarse murmuring thro' the thirsty sands.
Five zones she added. In mid place she kept
    With red distinct the lands

Leaguered with burnings; all the region showed
    Scorched into blackness, and the thread
Dry as with sunshine that eternal glowed;
    On either hand were spread

The realms of life, lapt in a milder breath
    Kindly to men: and next appear,
On this extreme and that, dull lands of death;
    She made them dark and drear

With year-long frost, and saddened all the hue
  With endless winter ; last she showed
What seats her Sire's grim brother holds, nor knew
  The fated dark abode.

THE DREAM-LOVERS.

[ATHENÆUS, xii. 35.]

O DATIS, child of him who ruled the lands
　　Eastward from Tanaïs, in her dreams beheld
Prince Zariadres, whom the tribes obeyed
To Tanaïs northwards from the Caspian Gates,
Beheld, and loved him ; and the Prince beheld
The maid in visions of the night, and loved,—
Fairest of Asian dames the girl, and he
Of Asia's sons the fairest. So the twain,
Though sundered far, were constant each to each.
And Zariadres, when the time was ripe,
Asked her in marriage ; but the King, whose house
But for the girl was childless, lest his realm
Should fret at alien rule, denied the suit ;
And ere the year had circled, he ordained

His daughter's marriage, calling to the feast
Kinsmen, and friends, and princes of the land,
All Scythia's noblest, nor for whom the bride
He purposed and the heirship of his crown
Declared ; but when the revel was at height
Bade fetch the maiden to the hall, and said,
' These be thy suitors, girl. Now take the cup,
The cup from which the Kings my fathers drank,
And mix, and give it as thy heart shall choose.'
With one swift glance from under drooping lids
She scanned the glittering throng, nor saw the One,
The lover of her dream ; then slowly turned,
And sought the board whereon the cups were ranged,
Seeing her instant fate, but hoping yet
Wildly against all hope. And he, it chanced,
Drawn by war rumours to his frontier, lay
Encamped by Tanaïs ; and he knew her need,
Though no man told him, for their hearts were one.
All day he drave across the Scythian plain,
Nor spared the lash, and when the sun was set

Came where the King held revel. There he left
Chariot and charioteer, nor feared to pass,
In garb of Scythian prince, the palace doors.
With shout and song the revellers quaffed the wine
Unheeding, and Odatis at the board
Stood cup in hand, and slowly mixed the draught,
While the big tear-drops trickled down her cheek.
Then the Prince knew the lady of his dreams,
And whispered, ' At thy bidding I am come,
O best beloved'; and she beheld him stand,
Unknown, yet known, and smiling through her tears,
Reached him her hand, nor doubted, and the twain
Passed from the hall to where the chariot stood.
Forth sprang the willing steeds, and all the night,
For Aphrodite gave them strength, devoured
The plain with feet untiring, till they came
With morning to the river and the camp.

HECUBA AND AGAMEMNON.

Euripides, *Hecuba*, 774-833.

NOW, for the cause for which I clasp thy knees,
    Listen, and if thou deemest that my wrongs
Are justly borne, I bear and am content;
But else, O King! avenge me of the man,
This wickedest of hosts, who neither fears
The nether world, nor upper, and hath wrought
The wickedest of deeds; for many a time
He sat among my guests and ever stood
First of my friends, and so received my son
In wardship, with provision as was meet;
Then slew him; aye! and having slain, denied
Due burial rites, but cast him on the waves.

For me—I am a slave, and doubtless weak;
Yes—but the gods are strong, and strong is law,
Which sways the gods, for verily of law
Comes faith in gods that rule us, and the sense
By which we live, dividing right from wrong.
Shall law appeal to thee, and be contemned?
Shall he who slays the guest, who robs the shrine,
Escape unpunished? Nay, for then would be
No justice anywhere in human things.
Far be such baseness from thee! yield me, King,
The suppliant's meed of pity; stand apart,
As stands a painter, and regard me well,
And know what woes are mine. But yesterday
I was a queen, I am thy slave to-day;
I had a noble offspring, see me now
Childless and old—no fatherland, no friends—
Surely the wretchedest of mortal things.

         [Agamemnon seems to be about to depart.

Unhappy that I am! where wilt thou go?
I seem to speak but vainly, woe is me!

O foolish mortals, why do we pursue,
Careful, as duty bids, all arts beside,
But this one art—Persuasion—though it be
Sole lord of men, desire not with desire
E'en at a price to learn, and so to sway
All hearts to what we would, and gain our end?
Who after me can hope for happy days?
So many sons I had, and all are gone,
And I am borne away in shameful guise,
A captive of the spear, and see the smoke
Rising above this city of my birth.

 * * * * * * *

Listen again. Thou seest this dead child ;
Pay him due honour, 'tis to thine own kin
Honour is paid. One word is lacking yet.
Oh ! that there dwelt within these arms a voice
(The work of art, Dædalean or divine),—
These hands, and these white hairs, and weary feet,
All should together cling about thy knees
With tears, with all imaginable speech.

O Lord! chief light of Hellas, hear, and reach

A hand of helping to my helpless age,—

Aye, though I be as nothing, reach it forth.

Still should the good man serve the cause of Right,

And to ill-doers work continual ill.

'COULD WE FORGET THE WIDOWED HOUR.'

TENNYSON, *In Memoriam* xxxix.

HEI mihi! si nobis orbata intercidat hora,
    si liceat carum sic meminisse caput,
ut sponsam meminisse iuvat quo tempore crines
    virgineos proprio flore ligavit Hymen!
illa, suis iam fausta precantibus omnia, notos
    supremum alloquitur mox abitura locos,
dum desiderium teneros leve turbat ocellos,
    spesque simul, vernum ut sol pluviaeque diem.
gaudia nunc agitant animos incerta paternos,
    matris et humectat lacrima multa genas,
filia dum longo complexu avulsa suorum
    quaerit quae potior foedera iungit amor.
illi pars alere et praeceptis fingere prolem,
    et fungi quae lex munera fasque iubet,

iungere praesentes annis venientibus annos,
    et sobolem veteri consociare novam.

tu quoque iam peragis, credo, felicius aevum,
    quodque facis nunquam mors abolebit opus;

tu quoque caelicolum iam viribus auctus adultis
    officio fungi nobiliore potes.

at tua sors illi quantum heu! diversa videtur;
    gaudebit quotiens, sit procul illa, domus,

prospera sollicitas cum fama advenerit aures!
    et quotiens, patrios cum petet ipsa focos!

illic saepe novam prolem ostentare iuvabit,
    saepe suis placeat quod didicisse loqui,

dum, dolor amissae si cui prius acrior esset,
    ipse novas pariter res placuisse ferat.

at nos, donec hyemps hanc clauserit ultima vitam,
    fata vetant caras consociare manus.

heu! ego quos novi perlustro flebilis agros,
    tu loca mortali non adeunda pedi.